How the Elephants
Saved Christmas

Written by Linda L. Olson
Illustrated by Greta Gretzinger

© Copyright 2007 by Linda L. Olson

Illustrator: Greta Gretzinger

Library of Congress Number: 2006905793

ISBN 978-1-4243-4044-6

This is a work of fiction. Names, characters, places and incidents either are the product of the author's imagination or are used fictitiously. Any resemblance to actual persons (living or deceased), events or locales is entirely coincidental.

Printed in China.

To order additional copies of this book, visit your local bookseller or contact:

Gold Star Press

P.O. Box 1688

Wilson, Wyoming 83014

www.goldstarpress.com

307-690-5626

No one saw the meteor as it shot through the sky over central Africa early in the morning of December 25th. It was only 3:00 a.m., and the people in the cities and villages were sound asleep. They missed the beauty of this falling star streaking a silver path across the black sky.

Even Santa Claus had dozed off as his sleigh rocked gently through the darkness. It had been a long and busy night for Santa and his reindeer, and they had but one last stop to make in the small village of Menobi before heading back to the North Pole. Santa had fallen asleep dreaming about his soft slippers, his comfortable chair in front of a crackling fire, and a big mug of steaming hot chocolate. The reindeer were tired and longed to be in their warm barn. In the lead, Dasher and Dancer had closed their eyes and pretended they could smell the oats and hay as they pulled the sleigh toward the village.

3

So you see, neither Santa nor the reindeer saw the meteor coming. As it whooshed by—nearly hitting the back of the sleigh!—it upset the magical balance that held the sleigh and reindeer in the sky. The sleigh began to fall, pulling the reindeer behind it! The reindeer strained and stretched out their legs, trying to put the sleigh back on course. But they were very tired and they could not do it. Down, down, down the sleigh fell, until it landed—kerplop!—in the deep, squishy, sticky mud of a water hole on the grassy plains of central Africa.

4

The landing was hard, and Santa Claus nearly flipped out of the sleigh, but he managed somehow to hold on, and he kept his wits about him. Instead of jumping right out of the sleigh into the mud, Santa thought for a minute. Then, he stood on the seat of the sleigh and with a big heave, jumped to the dry land above the water hole. Santa ran to check on the reindeer.

"Dasher, Dancer, Prancer, Vixen, Comet, Cupid, Donner, Blitzen! Are you all right, unhurt?" Santa looked at each reindeer, and was relieved to read in their intelligent eyes that they had not been injured in the fall. In fact, Dasher and Dancer had all four feet on dry land. But Prancer and Vixen were in mud to their ankles; Comet and Cupid to their knees; Donner and Blitzen were nearly up to their hips in the gooey stuff; and the runners of the heavy sleigh were buried completely.

"Dasher, Dancer, all of you, can we pull the sleigh out of this mess?" asked Santa. They tried and tried. The reindeer strained against their harnesses, and Santa

pulled and tugged on harness straps. But it was no use. Santa Claus's sleigh and reindeer were stuck, and stuck good.

"Oh, no, oh no," Santa repeated over and over again as he paced back and forth on the dry land. "What are we going to do? What can we do? How did this happen? I wasn't paying attention, that's how. This is all my fault! Oh, reindeer, I'm so sorry. How will we get home before dawn? And you know what that means if we aren't home before daylight—NO MORE CHRISTMAS! What are we going to do? What are we going to do?"

Santa was very upset. So upset, in fact, that he disturbed the monkeys who had been sleeping in the trees on the opposite side of the water hole. First each monkey opened one eye, but when they saw the show going on in the mud, they opened both eyes and found a good place to scratch while they watched. Santa was very entertaining!

Then a nighthawk flew low over the trees while catching an insect to eat. The nighthawk was surprised to find the monkeys awake, and more surprised when they called to her, "Look! Look! Look!" She looked, saw Santa and the reindeer and the sleigh, and flew closer to look again. The nighthawk could not understand what Santa was saying, but she sensed that something was wrong. I must get Quiet One, she thought to herself, and she flew away into the night.

• • •

Time passed. Santa sat down on the bank of the water hole and put his head in his hands. The reindeer's heads drooped in exhaustion and worry. When Santa looked up, an African boy stood before him. The boy was tall and lean, dressed in a dusty orange robe that slung over one shoulder. He wore his black hair long, and pulled back in a braid. His large dark eyes were full of caution and distrust as he watched Santa.

"Oh, oh thank goodness you've come! Can you help me? I really need your help—we're stuck, you see," Santa spoke quickly in his relief. "Are there men in your village who could get my reindeer and sleigh out of this mud? It's very important that we get out!"

The boy stood motionless, watched, and said nothing.

Santa stopped, put his hand to his forehead, and tried to stand still. "I'm sorry. I suppose this looks very strange to you, young man. Let me introduce myself—I am Santa Claus."

The boy said nothing.

Santa thought for a moment. "Ah, let me see. Perhaps here in Africa you know me by a different name. Pere Noel, perhaps? St. Nicholas?"

At last the boy spoke, softy, so that Santa had to strain to hear him. "I have heard of St. Nicholas: the saint of children who brings them happiness on the Christian holiday called Christmas."

"Yes, yes!" nodded Santa.

"I do not believe in you," said the boy.

"Oh, dear me, dear me. Well, I'm real, all right. I live at the North Pole, where there is snow all year. And on Christmas Eve I travel around the world answering the wishes of children. Here, touch my coat. Who else would be wearing a heavy red fur suit in Africa? See, here are the reindeer and my sleigh. It's nearly empty now, because I have been delivering presents all night. In fact, this was to be my last stop."

The boy listened, then turned away, heading back into the African night.

"No! Please stay!" cried Santa. "If I can't get home before dawn, there will be no more Christmas! The magic will be gone forever! Think of the children around the world who count on me every year! Think of Suli!"

At the mention of that name, the boy turned back to Santa. "Suli?" he asked.

"Yes, yes. Suli and all the children of the village of Menobi. It was my last stop this year. But I guess Suli won't get a visit from me now, or ever," Santa sighed.

"I know Suli. She is the daughter of the headman of the village." The boy was quiet for a moment, thinking. Then he looked at Santa and said, "I will help you." He turned, and whistled into the night. A yearling African elephant appeared out of the darkness and came to the boy's side. He scratched her trunk affectionately, then turned to Santa.

"This is Kayla. My name is Katanga, but the villagers call me Quiet One." Then the boy talked quickly and lowly to the elephant. She turned, threw her trunk

14

up into the air, and trumpeted once, twice, three times, a sound that shattered the stillness of the African night. "Now we wait," said Katanga, as he seated himself on the ground.

Santa was amazed. He sat down beside the boy, then said, "Well, now, Katanga. You certainly have a way with that elephant. Do you also live in Menobi?"

"No. I have left the villages forever. I live with the elephants," answered Katanga. He hesitated, then turned to look Santa in the eyes.

"My father was killed by bad men when he tried to stop them from killing the elephants. That was two years ago. Now I try to keep the elephants safe from the poachers, and Suli helps me. She cannot come out onto the plains because her leg has been crippled since she was born. But she is brave. When she hears the poachers talking with her father, offering money to the village if his men will help them find the elephants, Suli talks to me with the drums. She warns me, and I move the elephants to safety."

"I see," said Santa. Then he added, "I believe you are both very brave."

They fell silent, and waited. Suddenly, Katanga broke the silence. "Tell me about the snow."

"Snow? Oh, well, yes, I suppose you've never had a chance to play in the snow. Let me see. . . it's very white and soft and cold. Sometimes it's fluffy like feathers, but other times it's hard enough to walk on. There's nothing more lovely than newly fallen snow, and it tastes like the sweetest water you can imagine."

Katanga frowned, trying to visualize Santa's words. Unsuccessful, he shook his head and sighed, "I would like to see the snow."

The silence came again. Santa glanced worriedly at the eastern horizon where the faintest glow of light had begun to push back the black blanket of night. "Not enough time, not enough time," he mumbled. He put his hands on the ground to change his position and felt the earth beneath them tremble. Startled, he looked at Katanga. Quiet One smiled faintly, then whispered, "Machu comes."

Soon Kayla shuffled her feet and grunted a welcome. Slowly Santa began to see the outline of a huge beast—at least five times the size of the yearling elephant—coming toward him and the boy, shaking the ground with each step. Santa scrambled to his feet as the outline filled out, showing him a dark gray bull elephant. The huge animal came to a stop a few feet in front of Katanga, towering over the young boy. His tusks, nearly four feet in length, gleamed dully in the moonlight.

"This is Machu, the only big bull left in Kayla's herd. He is the one who will help you," Katanga said simply as he stroked the elephant's trunk.

"Good gracious," spluttered Santa, "I've never seen anything like him. He's enormous!" Santa started toward the elephant, then hesitated. "Is he friendly?"

"Friendly?" Katanga paused for a moment. "He is wise, loyal, strong and brave. He is angry and mistrustful, too. But friendly? No, I would not call him friendly."

Katanga tapped Machu's trunk, and the elephant lifted the boy and perched him high up on his neck. Katanga leaned forward and spoke softly in Machu's ear for several seconds. Then, the big elephant moved to the mudhole and the stuck sleigh.

Santa guessed what Machu would try to do, and ran to Dasher and Dancer, hoping the reindeer could help pull the sleigh out.

Machu raised his trunk and used it to feel the sleigh, then slowly waded into the water hole behind it. Holding his trunk high so that he could breathe, he slid his long tusks into the mud and under the trapped sleigh. Then, he heaved upward, neck muscles straining. The sleigh didn't budge. Machu heaved again, and the sleigh moved an inch. Santa called to the reindeer to pull, pull! When Machu tried again, pushing upward with all of his great elephant strength, the sleigh suddenly popped out of the mud, followed by Donner and Vixen, then Comet and Cupid. In

seconds, all were on dry ground. Machu trumpeted his success to the skies.

Santa ran around the sleigh and reindeer, determining that everything was unhurt. "Oh, thank you, thank you, thank you!" he babbled as he readied the sleigh to take to the sky. Then, collecting himself, he bowed low to the boy and the elephant. "Thank you, Machu. Thank you, Katanga. With all my heart I thank you," he said solemnly. "Now I must be off. The sun comes!"

But before Santa could jump into the sleigh, the rumble of drums broke the stillness of the night.

Katanga froze. "It's Suli," he murmured while he listened to the message she was sending. "Oh, no! The poachers! They're coming! Now!" Katanga looked at Santa with frightened eyes, knowing what would happen to the elephants. "They must have heard Kayla and Machu. I must get them away!" He looked for the big bull and found him wading into the waterhole to drink and wash the mud from his body. "Machu, no! You must go!"

Santa glanced at the brightening horizon, then turned to Katanga. "You get the elephants out of here. Leave the poachers to me." And with that, he sprang into the sleigh and whistled to Dasher and Dancer. The sleigh began to move forward, and in seconds lifted into the sky.

Santa and the reindeer flew toward the village, and soon they could see three vehicles full of men and guns coming quickly along a dusty track across the plains. Santa looked and saw a place where the track crossed a dry streambed, just a short distance ahead of the poachers. "That's the place, Dasher," he called. "Steady now, and DOWN, REINDEER!"

The reindeer and sleigh streaked from the sky toward the approaching vehicles. The driver of the first one saw something coming, blinked and rubbed his eyes. He looked again just in time to get a close up view of Dancer's wet nose and an earful of jingling bells. In a panic he swerved the wheel, driving his vehicle into the streambed and forcing the other two vehicles to swerve to avoid hitting him. Two of them turned over, and one hit a large rock.

Santa pulled the reindeer up, banked a turn, and made one more pass by the now stranded poachers. One of the men was raising a rifle toward him! Hurriedly, Santa waved his arm and called, "Guns to something else!" The poacher was surprised to find that he was holding a large candy cane! Santa had turned all of the guns into his favorite Christmas candy.

"Good work, reindeer," Santa called to the reindeer. "Serves them right, I say. I bet they don't even believe in Santa Claus—but maybe they will now! Back to Katanga, Dasher!"

Santa found the elephants again, Katanga atop Machu with Kayla trotting to keep up with the big bull. The rest of the herd was just visible in the distance.

"It's all right now, Katanga. We took care of them," Santa called as the sleigh hovered a few feet above the ground beside Machu.

"Now it is our turn to thank you, St. Nicholas."

"No need, son. I believe we're even. Listen, Katanga, I don't have time to get to the village. Will you give these to Suli and the others for me?" He handed Katanga a sack of toys, including a beautiful doll, dressed in the ceremonial clothing of Suli's people. Then he gave him a strange lightweight metal contraption. Katanga frowned, but Santa spoke first. "It's a brace for her leg, Quiet One. Soon she will ride the elephants across the plains with you."

"Santa, you have brought Suli much happiness," Katanga said solemnly. "Now I do believe in you, too."

Santa laughed. "I must go. Take care, Quiet One, until we meet again. On Dasher, on Dancer ..." His voice trailed away as the sleigh climbed into the sky. Then Santa turned the reindeer again, and flew silently over the boy on the elephant. He waved his arm and whispered one word. Then, smiling, he was gone.

Katanga didn't see or hear Santa pass over his head. He jumped in surprise when he felt the tiny flecks of cold on his skin. Looking around, he found the air full of tiny white flakes. They were soft, cold, and beautiful. When he caught some on his tongue, they tasted like the sweetest water he'd ever known.

"Snow," whispered Katanga.

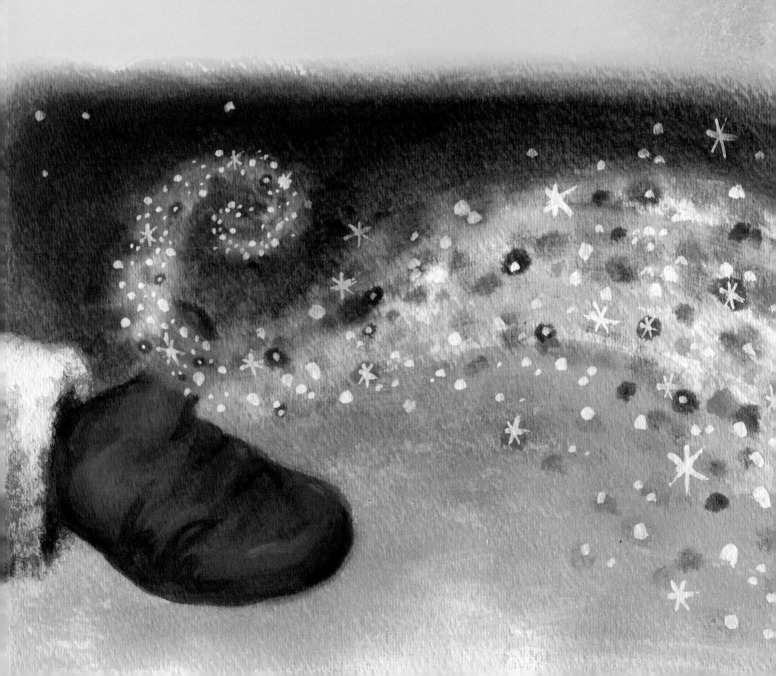

And then Quiet One laughed right out loud.